# Disney

# BEAUTY
## AND THE
# BEAST

*Belle's Story*

studio fun

# From the Author

I have always been a girl who loves books. And I've never stopped dreaming of adventure. So when my very own life became an amazing adventure of its own, my first thought was that I should write it all down, as it would surely make a splendid story.

My tale is full of peril, transformation, dramatic battles, mystery, enchantment, romance, and (in the best traditions of fairy tales) a happy ending.

But unlike the fairy tales of old, my story is true—I lived it!

Even now, I can remember each moment of my journey vividly . . .

When I was very young, I lived with my dear father in a cottage on the edge  of a town called Villeneuve. Although I was born in Paris, my father had moved us to the countrysi when I was still a baby, and the village was the only real home I'd ever known. I knew every buildin every cobblestone on the street, every villager. The were almost like family to me, although I confess that not all of us got along very well.

The village's friar, Père Robert, was jolly and kind, always willing to lend a hand (or a book!). He shared my love of the written word, and generously tolerated my pestering him for new material a few times a month.

The potter, Monsieur Jean, seemed to have his mind on his work, which sometimes made him a bit forgetful of other things. Still, he was as down to earth as the clay he used to make his wares.

**Agathe,** the town beggar, did whatever she could to get by, and I admired her for her resourcefulness. Even

though father and I were by no means wealthy, I tried to make sure I always had a little something for her.

The fishmonger, **Madame Clothilde** had a sharp tongue, and an even sharper eye for business. I'd seen her reduce grown men to tears with a glare. I always tried to be polite to her—to do otherwise was to risk a stern lecture, which I did not always have the patience to avoid contradicting.

What could I say about **Monsieur Baker?** His baguettes were so scrumptious! But he was a tough one to bargain with. He certainly knew which side of his bread was buttered.

I found the school's headmaster disagreeable, as he did not believe girls had a place in the classroom.

A ridiculous notion, as I am living proof that girls are every bit as capable as boys in whatever they put their minds to!

Monsieur Gaston was a soldier in the war, having earned the rank of captain. After returning to Villeneuve, he spent many of his days hunting, though I daresay his favorite

activity was flirting with the village lasses. Not that I think they had any complaints, exactly . . .

Monsieur LeFou . . . well, I'm not sure what he did, aside from tag along with Monsieur Gaston and do whatever he asked, poor man.

Safe, quiet, and familiar, that is Villeneuve in a nutshell. It was a good life, but a very small one. Though my neighbors found contentment in their daily chores and tasks, I often found myself longing for more.

My father taught me to read when I was very young, and from then on I devoured every book I could find. While I never quite felt like I fit in with the townspeople, I found a kindred spirit in Père Robert. We shared a deep love of literature. Though his collection of stories was meager, he graciously shared his books with me. Within the well-worn pages, I could venture beyond the borders of Villeneuve, and become lost in worlds unlike my own, encountering shipwrecked sailors marooned on tropic isles, gallant knights astride their noble steeds, and star-crossed lovers bound to a great destiny.

The books made my small corner of the world feel much bigger, and with every page I turned, I wished my story could be more like theirs. I yearned for adventure, and knew in my heart that one day I would find it. (Little did I know, adventure would find me, and much sooner than I ever expected . . . )

One day, I will travel to Paris!

My mother
used to
say this.

In provincial Villeneuve, gossip was the main source of entertainment—and my papa and I were frequently popular topics of discussion. My mother had died in Paris when I was an infant, and I often heard the village women despair of my father's ability to raise a girl properly on his own. They would remark that he was spoiling me by letting me wander so freely and read to my heart's content.

Fortunately, my father and I were as unconcerned with my "unladylike" behavior as the citizens were scandalized. An artist and inventor by trade, my father made a living by creating ingenious music boxes he sold at market once a year. He was very clever, and by virtue of his hard work we had made a pleasant enough life for ourselves in the village.

In what little spare time he had, Papa painted. My favorite of his works was the one he was least satisfied with: my mother, holding an infant girl—me—with one arm, a single red rose in her other hand.

I gathered from what little my father was able to tell me that my temperament is very similar to my mother's. "Free spirited," Papa called us. It seemed to make him happy that I was so much like her, but also deeply sad in some ways. I could tell he missed her terribly, and despite my urging, he would rarely speak of her. The merest hint of the subject seemed to cause him such pain that I never pressed too hard.

It's strange to think how it was one of my father's market trips that led to the adventure that would change my life so drastically. That morning, I helped my father pack and prepare the wagon for his overnight journey. I made sure he wa dressed properly for the weather and had everythin he needed. Before we bid each other our fond goodbyes, he asked me what I would like him to bring me from the market. It was something of a tender joke between us. I asked for the same thing each year—a single rose, like the one my mother held in the painting. It was a gift he'd never once failed to deliver. As I watched my father's wagon vanish dow the road, I had no expectation that this excursion would be any different than the ones before.

While my father was away on his trip, I had my own chores to attend to, and I set to them like the inventor's daughter I was. With the help of an old barrel, a leather strap, and the potter's mule, I was able to devise a way to get the laundry done very quickly—allowing me time to indulge in the pleasures of a good book. Or at least, that was the intent . . .

# MARKET!

*Henri's*
*Embroidered Cloaks*

*Maurice's*
*Music Boxes*

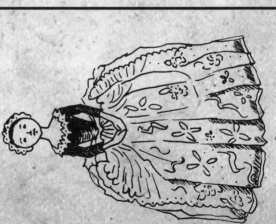

*Pierre's*
*Wooden Dolls*

**Guillaume's Knives**

**Antoine's Tapestries**

**Jean's Candles**

COME TO THE **ARTISAN**

I was sitting at the fountain, lost in the pages of my latest loan from Père Robert. It took me a moment to realize I was not alone. I looked up to see the eyes of a young village girl watching me. She asked what I was doing. I knew that the village headmaster did not allow girls in his classroom—was it possible she had never seen anyone reading for pleasure before? I replied that I was reading a story. Then I offered to teach her. I saw her eyes light up, and it made me remember how I felt when I first learned to read. It was like getting the keys to a secret door that unlocked the world.

She was more than willing, and eagerly listened as we began the lesson.

We were so absorbed in our impromptu instruction that I didn't notice the small crowd that had gathered—until I heard a voice rudely demand, "What do you think you are doing?" It was the school's headmaster. He had apparently taken umbrage with my decision to teach a girl to read. Several other villagers, including Madame Clothilde, had turned out to watch the argument and offer their own (disapproving) opinions. I didn't understand the outrage—why shouldn't a girl be allowed to learn? What was wrong with that?

Apparently, they also did not wish a girl to
argue with them. Instead of engaging with me in a
conversation, they dismantled my machine, took my
barrel of laundry, and emptied it onto the street.
Then they chastised the girl for listening to me
and ushered her back inside the home where she
worked. I was left to gather my soggy laundry and
trudge back toward my cottage, infuriated and
disheartened by the events of the day.

I have to say that my spirits were not lifted
on the path home by the appearance of Monsieur
Gaston, who had caught wind of my troubles and
insisted on offering his opinion (unwanted and
unneeded, I must say). Although I considered him
more or less harmless, his pushy, boorish behavior
often put me on my guard. I could tell he saw me
as a challenge to be conquered instead of a person.

Our conversation took a decidedly unpleasant
turn when he informed me that the only children
I should concern myself with were my own."

I bristled at his implication, inferring he meant the children he wished we would have together. He didn't ask what I thought about his plan, of course, but I made my position clear. I told him in no uncertain terms that I wasn't at all ready for marriage or children—and that I would never marry him. I managed to make my excuses and escape home, closing the door in Gaston's face, trying to shake the weight of other people's ambitions and expectations from my shoulders. I had ambitions of my own.

The night passed uneventfully, and the next morning, the sun had only just come up when I heard the distinctive whinny of our old horse, Philippe. I was thrilled, thinking that Papa was safely back from his trip—but when I looked up, expecting to see him coming through our garden gate, I saw Philippe alone and wild-eyed.

I realized with horror that something must have happened to Papa on the road. Without thinking twice I leapt astride Philippe and whispered to him to take me to Papa. He seemed to understand me, for we whirled and galloped into the woods.

Philippe took us a long, long way. I had never
ventured so far outside of Villeneuve before.
Eventually, I was lost. I put my trust in Philippe,
thinking only of Papa, praying he would be all
right when we reached him.

Next to a broken tree stump, I spied my
father's overturned cart on the road, and I urged
faithful Philippe onward, my heart in my throat.
I was so worried that I hardly noticed as the dirt
beneath Philippe's hooves turned to snow, and my
breath began to crystalize in the air in front
of me.

Then I saw it—a great castle looming suddenly through the trees. Wreathed in winter, the crumblin' spires black against the stars, it was a sight I can never forget.

In the back of my mind, I knew it was strange. I'd never heard tales of a castle near Villeneuve, and it hardly seemed the sort of thing that would pass unremarked by the village. It was straight out of a book of fairy tales—so out of place that I felt as if I were stepping into another world. But Philippe stood solidly beside me in the courtyard, pawing at the ground insistently and whinnying. I knew my Papa must surely be there . . . and if he was in that strange place, then I had to go inside and find him.

I picked up a heavy branch, not knowing what I would find inside and wanting to be prepared if I had to defend myself. I walked up the steps, shivering in the cold that until then I'd barely noticed. I pushed at the castle doors. To my surprise, they were unlocked, and swung open at my touch. The castle interior was as strangely derelict as the outside—everything covered in a thick layer of dust, the furnishings in great disrepair. I could see no sign of my father, but gathered up my courage and tightened my grip on the branch, determined to keep looking until I found him.

As I moved deeper into the castle, I swore I heard whispers echoing through the impossibly long, dark hallways, and I could feel unseen eyes on me. I called out, hoping that someone would come with whom I could appeal, argue, question . . . someone who would make this situation make sense! But no one answered. For a moment I wondered if I had fallen from my horse and struck my head, for this seemed more like a dream than reality. Telling myself that surely there was an explanation for all this, I picked up a candelabrum to light my way.

I have no idea how I eventually made my way to the castle's upper reaches, only that I did, and that my father must have heard me calling, for I heard his voice, though it was distant at first. I followed it through many cold, stony passageways until at last I arrived at a locked cell door.

I saw Papa huddled inside—the look on his face told clearly of his shock to see me in such a place. I could tell that he was dreadfully ill—his skin pale and his voice raspy as he spoke to me.

He urged me to flee, saying that the castle was alive and "he" would find me if I stayed. I thought perhaps he was hallucinating from fever, but before I could try to open the door, there was a dreadful, heart-stopping roar. I spun around and swung with my branch . . . .

. . . and struck nothing.

But I could see that someone was there,
a great figure in the shadows, lurking and
pacing. My father's captor. The meager light
only served to make the shadows deeper, but
I clutched my improvised weapon tighter,
demanding my father's release.

A deep, growling voice came back, accusing
my father of thievery. He had stolen a rose
from the castle's garden.

# My heart became ice.

Papa had only been thinking of me, of my
request, which seemed petty and foolish now.
I replied that the rose had been for me, that
it was my punishment to serve, not Papa's. I
demanded the mysterious captor imprison me
instead, and when he would not show himself,
I thrust the candelabrum into the shadows
to reveal . . .

a Beast.

There truly was no other way to describe him—a Beast. He was all horns and claws and hair, and stared at me with intense eyes that were strangely proud and human.

could hardly breathe. I could hardly think. Through a mouthful of terrifyingly sharp teeth, the Beast demanded I choose who would stay—my father or me.

Papa begged me to reconsider. He refused to let me take his place, telling me to live my life and forget him. I knew I could not change his mind, and so I agreed to leave. (At least, that was what I wanted my father to believe.) Leaving him was an impossible request—I knew he would not survive the Beast's dark, cold cell much longer. I would not leave my father at the creature's mercy. I persuaded the Beast to open the door to my father's cell, and rushed to his side. Wrapping him in my arms, I whispered, "I will escape, I promise." Then I turned on my heel and pushed him through the door toward the Beast. I heard Papa shout a protest, even as the door slammed shut behind him. I begged the Beast not to hurt Papa as he was dragged away.

No matter how I tried to tell myself that my decision was for the best, that I would escape, and reunite with my father very soon, I still feared that I was quite in over my head. I sank to the cold stone, wrapped my arms around my knees, and began to cry.

I was completely . . . alone.

Except I was not alone. Shortly after the Beast left, the cell door clicked open. A voice called out to me cheerfully, announcing that I was to be escorted to my room. Questions filled my hea My room? Am I not going to be kept in the tower? Who is speaking to me?

Expecting a castle guard, I grabbed a small stool and demanded the speaker show himself. I readied myself to attack and escape. Imagine my shock when light spilled across my cell's floor, revealing a candelabrum, who bowed and greeted me pleasantly. It was all simply too much. I couldn't help it. I screamed and struck with the stool, quenching the candelabrum's flames and leaving us both in darkness.

Fortunately the candelabrum rekindled himself swiftly and introduced himself as Lumiere. He was joined an instant later by a mantel clock named Cogsworth. Both of them moved, walked, spoke—undeniably alive. They insisted I follow them, and because this request was no more bizarre or alarming than anything else I had encountered that day, I did as they asked.

As I was led to my new room (listening to Lumiere and Cogsworth argue with each other every step of the way), I took the opportunity to better examine my surroundings. The castle was gigantic, and as we crossed a raised, narrow footbridge that led briefly outside, I got a proper sense for how enormous the grounds were. The winter woods that surrounded them also seemed endless. I could not even begin to guess in which direction Villeneuve was.

When we reached "my" room, I braced myself for more shredded draperies and crumbling finery, but for once, I was _pleasantly_ surprised. The room was opulence itself—beautifully appointed and everything as bright and beautiful as though it ha been decorated the day before. Seemingly satisfied Lumiere and Cogsworth left me alone with the room's other inhabitant, Madame de Garderobe. She took it upon herself to put me at my ease by constructing a terribly uncomfortable dress for me—so stuffed with fabric and ribbon that it could stand quite easily on its own. She then promptly fell asleep.

Truly alone at last, and now apparently unguarded, I thought that perhaps I had a chance to escape.

# MY MAP OF THE CASTLE

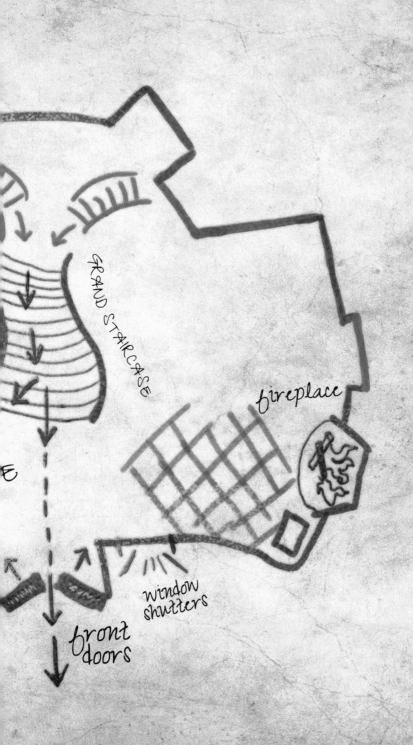

GRAND STAIRCASE

fireplace

window
shutters

front
doors

BALLROOM

X

ENTRANC
HALL

window
shutters

Without a moment's hesitation I began deconstructing the dress that Madame de Garderobe had made for me. While it failed as a comfortable dress, it proved to be a more than satisfactory source of raw material for an escape out the window. I was confident I could make a rope long enough to descend to the ground from my tower room. Of course, after that, I would have to get Philippe, journey back through the snowy woods, and somehow find my way back to Villeneuve . . . but I could not, did not allow myself to hesitate.

I was testing the distance I still had to go when there was a loud knock at the door. I nearly jumped out of my skin at the sound, and was further unnerved when the voice of the Beast sounded . . . inviting me to dinner. I nearly laughed out loud at the absurdity. He had imprisoned my father, imprisoned me, and then he wanted me to sit down at a table with him as though we were old friends! I preferred to go hungry.

Ways to escape the castle:

Feign illness, escape when the door opens?

Hide behind the door and run out while they're looking for me.

Look for a secret passageway.
What kind of castle doesn't
have secret passageways?

~~Jump from the window.~~
              No, it's far too high!

Make a rope, climb down from window.

He did not take my rejection well—not that I expected him to. He replied that I could go ahead and starve, for if I didn't eat with him, I would not eat at all. I heard him storm off, and I breathed a sigh of relief. I dreaded him bursting in and discovering my planned method of escape.

The rope was
nearly done, the ribbons
and torn scraps of cloth
proving quite sturdy when
braided together. However,
I was interrupted again, this
time by a teapot named Mrs. Potts.
She bustled in and immediately spotted my rope
and deduced my plans—but rather than becoming
angry, she only offered me a cup of tea. I liked
her immediately, and as we chatted, she confirmed
my suspicions that the castle was under some sort
of enchantment. She insisted I not undertake an
escape on an empty stomach, and I allowed myself
to be persuaded to have dinner.

Dinner turned out to be dinner and
entertainment, with the emphasis firmly on the
entertainment. No sooner had I been seated at
one end of a ridiculously long dining table than
Maestro Cadenza, the harpsichord, struck up a
tune, and I was treated to what must have been
the entire population of the castle pulling out

all the stops for my entertainment. Spoons sang, forks danced, napkins swung from chandeliers! My mouth fell open as all around me corks popped and beautiful plates piled high with delectable-looking food whirled past. I've never seen anything so magnificent, so dazzling, not even in my wildest dreams. It was a feast for the eyes . . . unfortunately, not for the stomach. Every dish I tried to sample danced out of reach before I could touch it—every utensil spun out of my grip before it could be used. It seemed they were so excited to entertain they had quite forgotten that a dinner guest needed to actually be able to eat the food.

The servants I met at dinner were all so different, but invariably helpful and kind They all tried so hard to make me feel welcome.

Lumiere, the candelabrum, was a footman in the castle, and well-loved by all the staff. Little surprise there, as his kindness and free-spirited personality had a way of lighting up any room.

Cogsworth, the castle's majordome was rather officious and grumpy on the face of things. However, deep in his gears beat a heart of gold, as he revealed himself to be kind-hearted and loyal over time.

Mrs. Potts, the housekeeper of this grand estate, and her little son Chip treated me like family from the first day I found myself in the castle. Their companionship and understanding warmed my hear even on the coldest nights.

Plumette, the head maid, was a bit flighty, but always there to dust up any messes the other inhabitants left behind—and she and Lumiere were obviously old flames.

Madame de Garderobe and her husband, Maestro Cadenza, were once renowned performers. Although limited to a smaller stage in their enchanted state, the maestro still made beautiful music, and the madame had a way of bringing a certain diva flair even to her new role as a bedroom wardrobe.

Chapeau, one of the castle's valets, never spoke, but he found other ways to be expressive, and somehow never had any trouble making his feelings known.

My curiosity was now well and truly piqued about the castle and its inhabitants. Escape could wait for a few hours more. I had been warned earlier about the castle's West Wing; Cogsworth told me it was the one place where I was forbidden to go. I had no intention of obeying this directive— indeed, if I was going to find answers, the West Wing seemed like the most likely place to start. Mustering my courage, I made my way there.

As I walked into the West Wing, I found myself surrounded by deliberate destruction and disarray. It seemed clear that the Beast's temper had been at work in these rooms, as the furnishings were shredded and scattered. There was also some sort of "nest" on the floor made of blankets and torn-up pillows. I jumped when I thought I saw someone standing behind a curtain—then relaxed when I realized it was only an oil painting.

With caution, I picked my way through the rubble toward it, and saw that it was a family portrait, a king, a queen, and a prince. Parts of the portrait had been torn beyond recognition, but the eyes of the prince were strikingly familiar . . .

I was distracted from my musings by an odd light. I walked toward it and saw a single rose, floating as if by magic. Mesmerized, I reached out to touch the glass that encased it.

A shadow fell across my body and a terrifying roar sent a shock up my spine. The Beast had returned. (Had he ever left? Had he been watching me from the shadows?) His outrage and fury were palpable as his paws closed around the rose's container and checked to ensure I had not harmed it.

He turned on me, his voice loud enough to shake the stones around us, and I thought he was certainly angry enough to harm me. Cogsworth had been right—I should not have gone there.

As the Beast lashed out with his claws, sending a column crumbling to the ground, he shouted for me to get out. I fled down the stairs, berating myself for thinking of anything but escaping.

I had to go—I had to get home to my father and leave this cursed place behind.

I found my way outside and located the stables and faithful Philippe—who seemed as ready to flee as I was. I threw myself onto his back, and together we rode out of the castle courtyard and blindly into the woods. I only hoped that he could remember the way back, as I was too rattled to think of anything but getting as far away as possible.

I was relieved when it seemed we had not been followed, but as my eyes adjusted to the darkness, I could see flickering shapes in the woods around us. A howl sounded out of the darkness. Not the howl of the Beast, but the howl of a hungry wolf.

Before long I could see them clearly. Not one, but a whole pack of wolves—a dozen at least—hungry and vicious and getting closer with every moment. We ran on and on, through the woods, across a frozen pond, but they pursued.

## Suddenly they were upon us, snapping at Philippe's legs.

He bucked, and I leapt from his back and into a soft snowbank.

I looked for something to defend myself.
Spotting a large branch, I picked it up and swung
it wildly at the first wolf I saw. It yelped on
impact, but another wolf seized the branch in
its jaws and yanked it from my fingers. I looked
into the eyes of another advancing wolf and
remembered the stories where a heroine had to
face down her enemies alone and unprotected.
But their stories always seemed to involve a
miraculous rescue or escape, and I could hope for
no such assistance . . .

. . . . or so I thought.

Suddenly the Beast was there, fighting the wolves off with a terrible, supernatural strength. As I huddled by Philippe in equal parts confusion and shock, I watched wolves surround the Beast. They tore at him with their long teeth. He shook them off, roared, and slashed at them with his own claws.

For a moment I thought he would be overwhelmed but the wolves were no match for him. Soon they fled, yelping, and disappeared into the dark woods.

For a moment the Beast stood triumphantly, his breath heavy and ragged, but then he sank to his knees in the snow. I could see deep wounds beneath his cloak, and knew that despite his strength and ferocity, the wolves must have injured him grievously.

I also knew that if I was going to escape, that was my moment. My captor could not stop me, I was not hurt, and the wolves had fled. But the Beast had nearly been killed saving my life. To leave him alone was unthinkable.

With great difficulty, I helped him onto Philippe's back, and we began the long, slow walk back to his castle.

When we made it back, the castle's inhabitants were frantic with worry upon seeing the Beast's injuries. With their help, I got him up to his bed, and set about tending to his wounds.

I knew a little about such things, having taken care of my father for so many years, but the Beast proved to be a very poor patient. He would flinch before I even touched him, and when I did touch him, he would complain that I was hurting him.

"If you held still, it wouldn't hurt as much," I pointed out. He shot back, "If you hadn't run away, none of this would have happened." I replied that it was his temper that had gotten us both into the who. mess, to which he had no satisfactory response. He sulked, but agreed to rest and slowly drifted to slee Beneath the Beast's fur and teeth and temper, I reflected, he was really more like a spoiled child than a monster.

Salve for the Beast's wounds:

Honey
Rosemary
Lamb's Ear Leaves

Heat rosemary and honey over
a low fire until fragrant.

Once cooled, apply to the wounds
and wrap with lamb's ear leaves
or boiled cloth dressings.

Change dressings daily.


As I watched him sleep, the staff thanked
me for saving him. I could not understand their
gratitude or their concern. From what I could
understand, he had cursed them somehow, and it
seemed to me that they were entirely blameless.
How could they still be so worried about him?

With reluctance, then, they began to tell
me their story.

Not so long ago, a handsome young prince lived in a beautiful castle. Although he had everything his heart desired, the prince was spoiled, selfish, and unkind.

The prince taxed the village to fill his castle with the most beautiful objects, and his parties with the most beautiful people.

One night, an unexpected intruder arrived at the castle, seeking shelter from the bitter storm. As a gift, she offered the prince a single rose.

Repulsed by her haggard appearance, the prince turned the woman away. But she warned him not to be deceived by appearances, for true beauty is found within. When he dismissed her again, the old woman's appearance melted away to reveal . . .

a
beautiful
Enchantress!

The prince tried to apologize, but it was too late. For she had seen that there was no love in his heart. As punishment, she turned him into a hideous beast, and placed a powerful spell on the castle and all who lived there.

As days bled into years, the prince and his servants were forgotten by the world, for the Enchantress had erased all memory of them from the minds of the people they loved.

But the rose she had offered
was truly an enchanted rose.
If the Beast could learn to
love another and earn their
love in return by the time the
last petal fell, the spell would
be broken. If not, he would be
doomed to remain a beast for
all time.

As the years passed, he fell
into despair and lost all hope.
For who could ever learn
to love a beast?

I was awed by their story. Of course I had no reason to doubt it—I was tending to the wounds of an enormous beast and speaking to furniture that spoke back. It was clear that every word was true.

But one thing still nagged at me. How could they still feel loyal to him, after his selfishness and pride had cursed them all?

They shared the Beast's troubled past. When he was a young boy, his beloved mother died, and afterward, his monstrous father raised him with a cruel and callous hand. His choices encouraged the prince to be cold and selfish, ultimately guiding him to his beastly fate. The staff blamed themselves for not intervening, but what could they have done against the will of a king?

I knew that the tragedy of his past didn't excuse his actions, but upon hearing his story, I felt sympathy for the Beast. Like me, he had lost his mother. But unlike me, he hadn't had a kind father to raise and guide him. I began to feel that I had misjudged him. There was obviously much more to his story than I had anticipated.

I learned one more truth that night.

Once the last petal of the enchanted rose fell, the Beast would be doomed to remain as he was, and the servants would become nothing more than lifeless objects.

I stayed near the Beast as he recovered over the next day. My voice seemed to soothe his fitful sleep, so I recited bits of books that I could remember—parts of old stories, sections of Shakespeare's plays. I nearly jumped out of my skin when I was idly reciting one of my favorite parts of A Midsummer Night's Dream and he joined in, perfectly finishing the stanza for me. When I told him Romeo and Juliet was my favorite play, he teased that he could find me something better to read than tragic romance.

Over my protests, he rose from bed and led me to the castle's library.

And such a library! Shelves stretched above my head, filled with more books than I had ever imagined could actually exist in the world!

I was so in awe that I almost didn't hear him tell me shyly, "If you like it so much, it's yours." I was stunned, but he seemed sincere. Something about the Beast had changed. He was being generous. Kind. Even funny. It was as if our brush with death had broken down some wall between us, and despite myself, I was charmed. Maybe . . . maybe I had been a bit hasty in my judgment.

The Beast's wounds still needed tending, so
we were seldom apart over the next few days.
I knew that without a careful eye watching him,
he doubtless would have made his injuries worse. It
was a surprising exchange of roles—previously he
had been my terrifying, severe captor. Then I was
looking after him, scolding him not to strain himself.
Even more surprising, he was willing to listen to
me! Although I still missed my father dearly, I was
caught up in the strange new pattern of life at
the castle.

There was much to do, and the days passed
easily. I rolled up my sleeves and helped the
staff clean some of the rooms, scrubbing floors
and windows until they gleamed.

I explored the castle library and found books I had only dreamed of reading. The Beast and I also shared meals together, and I began to appreciate his company. We shared a laugh when I caught him reading one of the tragic romances he'd so thoroughly teased me about before.

I could see how lonely his existence in the castle had been all those years. The staff had each other, but the Beast, lost in his guilt and regret and anger, had no one. I understood. After all, in Villeneuve, I had been an outcast, too.

The castle staff was very entertaining indeed. They said the funniest and wisest things. These are some of my dear favorites overheard during my time at the castle.

Lumiere: Look, Cogsworth. A beautiful girl.
Cogsworth: I can see it's a girl. I lost my hands, not my eyes.

Lumiere: 'Allo!

Lumiere: What do you want to be for the rest of your life, Cogsworth a man or a mantel clock?

Mrs. Potts: People say a lot of things in anger. It is our choice whether or not to listen.

Plumette: Lumiere, I grew three more feathers! And I just plucked yesterday.

Cogsworth: Oh no! It's—tick tock!—happening again—cuckoo! Pardon me.

Cogsworth: You know she will never love him.

Lumiere: A broken clock is right two times
a day, mon ami, and this is not
one of those times.

Mrs. Potts: I have found that most troubles
seem less troubling after a bracing
cup o' tea.

Lumiere: Checkmate. Again.

Cogsworth: Because you cheated. Again.

Mrs. Potts: The master's not as terrible as he
appears. Somewhere deep in his soul,
there's a prince of a fellow,
just waiting to be set free.

Cuisinier: Off! Off me while I work! Pepper,
get cracking! Salt, shake a leg!

One night, the Beast asked if I wanted to run away with him. The suggestion surprised me . . . until he showed me yet another enchanted object—a living atlas. Like the rose, it glowed with a golden, magic light, and I could see the ink moving on the page, mimicking waves lapping at distant shores and trees moving in a silent breeze. He told me I could travel anywhere I wished by touching its pages.

I didn't hesitate. I knew exactly where I wanted to go. I placed my hand on the page and closed my eyes. When I opened them, the Beast and I were standing in my parents' old home in Paris—a garret in a windmill.

It was the place I had been born and had seen every day in my father's paintings and every night in my dreams. But it was different, smaller, than I'd thought. It had fallen into disrepair and everything was covered in a thick layer of dust. It reminded me of the Beast's castle when I'd first arrived. It had the same feeling of neglect and emptiness.

I could feel my heart breaking as I surveyed the room that I'd so long romanticized. I spotted a rattle carved in the shape of a rose in the remains of my crib and picked it up.

Then the Beast spotted a strange object on a nearby chair and showed it to me. It was the birdlike mask of a plague doctor. So that was the truth—the plague had taken my mother. With growing sadness, I realized why my father had never told me the story of my mother's death, and why it still caused him so much pain. He had to leave her here, sick and dying, to keep me from perishing from the same terrible illness. There was nothing he could have done. But leaving my mother alone in her final moments must have shattered him.

...elling up in my eyes, and
... The Paris of my childhood was
...hinkingly, I reached out for the
...t's go home," I said, and to my
..., we both knew I meant the castle.

Later, the Beast proposed that we break-in the newly cleaned ballroom with a dance. I think he was kindly trying to take my mind off my sadness, and I appreciated the thoughtfulness. I was no longer the least bit frightened of the Beast—indeed, I thought of him almost as a friend. And yet why did I feel so nervous?

That night, Madame de Garderobe dressed me in a splendid gown that glistened with a dusting of gold. It flowed with my every move as I descended the grand staircase. There, the Beast was waiting, and he was resplendent. He was dressed in a handsome suit, his fur neatly groomed. We smiled somewhat timidly at each other, and I could tell we both felt a little strange. Still, we entered the ballroom arm in arm, and bowed to one another. I placed a hand on his shoulder, and he placed a gentle paw around my waist. And we danced.

How can I describe it? For all his bulk, the Beast was graceful and gentle, and he lifted me effortlessly. The ballroom around us glowed, and each moment felt like magic. It was as if nothing in the world existed but us. I couldn't explain my feeling of dizzying happiness. I only knew that there was something about the Beast, something about me that was different in a way that I couldn't express.

As the music wound down, we breathlessly made our way onto the terrace and into the cool night air. We gazed up at the stars as the Beast mused that it had been a long, long time since he'd last danced. Then he hesitated, as if wrestling with something. Finally, the words escaped his lips, "It's foolish, I suppose, for a creature like me to hope that one day he might earn your affections."

I felt a blush rising to my cheeks and my heart fluttered in my chest. I was taken off-guard by the question. I replied that I wasn't sure I could be happy at the castle if I wasn't truly free to come and go. I was fond of the Beast, but I confessed aloud that I still missed my father terribly. The Beast nodded soberly. A minute later he asked if I would like to see my father.

Without another word, he ushered me to his
room in the West Wing and gently handed me
another enchanted object—a mirror that would
show the one holding it whatever he or she asked.

"I wish to see my father," I told the mirror, expecting to see Papa sleeping in his bed, or puttering away in his workshop. Instead, I saw him in the village square. A crowd of angry villagers surrounded him and he looked disheveled and terrified. My heart sank. In that moment, nothing but Papa mattered to me.

"You must go to him," the Beast said, breaking the silence. I turned to look at him, stunned. He was letting me go. No conditions, no caveats. The Beast I first met would never have released me, but the noble, kind, and gentle Beast I'd come to know told me to go without a second thought. I started to give the mirror back to the Beast, but he bade me keep it so I would always have a way to see him.

Without another word, I tearfully left the castle, feeling deep gratitude and warmth toward the Beast. He was no longer my captor, but my friend.

I rode Philippe pell-mell through the woods and toward the village, dismounting only when I reached the village square. The villagers, led by Gaston, were locking my father inside a heavy wagon that would whisk him away to an asylum. I shouted for them to stop, and all eyes were suddenly on me. I heard whispers about my gown and my sudden appearance, but hardly paid them any mind as I strode forward to the wagon. My father was overjoyed to see me, but I could see that he was ill and hurt. I demanded that he be released immediately.

The villagers protested, saying that my father had been making unbelievable claims about a magic castle and a ferocious Beast—claims I knew were perfectly true. When I tried to tell them so, they scoffed. I saw they would not believe my words . . . but perhaps they would believe their own eyes. I pulled out the magic mirror, and held it aloft and shouted, "Show me the Beast!" An image appeared of the Beast, alone in his castle. Then I saw the fear in villagers' eyes at the Beast's monstrous appearance.

Gaston snatched the mirror from me, exclaimir that the Beast was evil and must be destroyed. I tried to tell the crowd that despite his appearance the Beast was a kind and gentle soul—as human as anyone. But they would not listen, especially when Gaston insisted that I must be under some sort of spell.

I could see a dangerous light in Gaston's eyes. As the villagers nodded and murmured, held sway by his words, I realized that I had underestimated him. Gaston was dangerous— far more than the Beast ever was—and he would stop at nothing to get his way.

"I say we kill the Beast!" He shouted with rage.

I tried to argue, to protest, but Gaston had the village in the palm of his hand. They were all too willing to take him at his word, and they locked me in the back of the asylum cart with my father to prevent me from warning the Beast they were coming. Helplessly, I listened as the villagers formed a bloodthirsty mob, rallying to attack the castle and kill the Beast.

I was horrified and heartbroken. The Beast was in danger of being killed, and it was my fault. Having come to know the Beast as I did, I had not thought about how frightening he might appear at first glance. It was my responsibility to save him. Watching through the barred window, I begged Papa to help me escape. He could not understand why I'd want to help the beast that imprisoned us both.

I showed Papa the carved rose rattle and his eyes filled with tears. I quickly explained how the Beast had taken me to the Paris of our past, how I had learned the truth about my mother, and how the Beast had let me go of his own free will. As I spoke, Papa realized I wasn't bewitched—no spell would have been able to reveal so much.

Using one of my hairpins, my father picked the lock, and together we escaped. I found Philippe still standing in the square. I tossed my ball gown to the ground, mounted Philippe, and we galloped out of the village toward the castle. I hoped against hope that I would be in time to save my friend.

I was terrified of what I would find when I returned. Would the castle be in flames? Would they have harmed my friends? Would I be too late to save the Beast? I raced through the woods at a breakneck pace, and arrived at the castle to find the aftermath of a battle. Villagers lay unconscious or groaning on the castle steps. Apparently the staff had been more than able to defend themselves against invaders.

I barely took the time to survey the damage.
The mirror had shown the Beast in the West
Wing—I knew that is where I would find Gaston
as well. I raced up the crumbling stairs with my
heart in my throat. I arrived on the rooftop just
in time to see Gaston raise his pistol and fire.

# Silently, the Beast fell.

I feared I was too late. But then I saw
Gaston ready his crossbow and realized that
the Beast must still be alive. There was hope!
Quickly, I took the arrows from his quiver.
When he reached for an arrow and found none,
Gaston whirled around to find me there. I broke
the arrows over my knee and tossed them away.
Then I lunged for his pistol. If the Beast was
alive, then I would make sure Gaston would
not have the chance to hurt him again. As we
struggled with the gun, Gaston lost his balance
and fell. I watched as he caught himself on a
lower level and swung out of sight.

I raced across the rooftops, determined to find the Beast. After several minutes of frantic scrabbling and clambering across loose tiles, I finally saw him—the Beast was on a faraway turret, hurt but alive. He was trying to maintain his grip on the crumbling stonework, and as I watched, he nearly slipped. "No!" I cried across the rooftop. His great shaggy head turned in my direction, spotting me.

"Belle!" he roared. "You came back!" The joy in his voice was palpable. He told me to stay where I was. He was coming for me.

I watched the Beast leap toward the West Wing, and despite his instruction for me to stay put, I hurried down the stairs to meet him. I stopped when I could see him through a window. The Beast was at the end of a footbridge not far from me. Suddenly, Gaston jumped out of nowhere wielding a great piece of stone spire. Gaston threw himself toward the Beast and struck him mercilessly on the back again and again.

The Beast roared in pain as he pushed past Gaston. I cried for Gaston to stop, but he would not. As the Beast reached the edge of the landing, he whirled on his attacker. In one motion, the Beast grabbed the club, and hurled it against the wall. Then he grabbed Gaston's throat with his great paw and lifted him off the ground, dangling him over the castle wall. I watched silently, my heart in my throat.

For a moment, I thought the Beast would drop Gaston to his death. But then I saw his expression change. Showing Gaston mercy, the Beast set him down. It was mercy I'd always known was in his heart. The Beast turned back to me, and with a single great leap, he cleared the distance between us, landing on the balcony before me. He had just enough time to flash me a confident, toothy smile.

Then a shot rang out.

It was Gaston. I ran toward the Beast, heedless of any danger. I watched in horror as Gaston, having recovered his pistol somehow, raised it again and fired the killing shot. Then the stones beneath his feet crumbled, and he fell. I heard a scream, then nothing. He was gone.

Numb, I reached the Beast's side, hoping against hope that the wound was not severe, that he would live. I cradled his head in my lap and ran my fingers through his hair, looking for the injury. I found it. It was grave, but perhaps . . .

The Beast rested his paw on my hand, gentle but firm. "You came back," he repeated, his breath ragged.

"Of course I came back. I'll never leave you again," I answered, my voice quivering.

"I'm afraid it's my turn to leave . . ." he whispered.

I refused to believe he was dying. We could not lose each other, not when I had only just realized . . . .

"At least I got to see you one last time," he rasped. His breathing grew softer, then stilled. His paw fell limply from my hand.

I could feel my heart breaking to pieces in my chest. "No . . . please . . . no!" I cried. I bent over his body, willing the Beast to move again, to breathe. Aloud, I begged him not to leave me. I could not imagine my life without him. I sank down, pressed my lips to his forehead, and whispered . . .

"I love you."

No sooner had those words left my mouth than I felt something strange begin to happen. I opened my eyes to see a golden light surround the Beast, beautiful and blinding. I watched as the light lifted him from my arms. I rose to my feet and stared in astonishment at the dazzling aurora of enchantment that made the very air around us crackle.

I shaded my eyes as the light grew to an almost intolerable brightness. Then the shape that was the Beast settled gently back to earth and faded to reveal . . .

. . . a man. A young man, handsome and familiar. He stared down at himself, then looked up at me, and when our eyes met, I knew.

I raced toward him. My tears of grief became tears of joy as I caressed his face, his hair . . . it was him. Undeniably, unbelievably him. There were no words, nothing that I could possibly think to say. Instead, he took me in his arms, pulled his face toward mine, and in that perfect moment, we kissed.

We were so thoroughly distracted that we didn't notice the transformations happening all around us. The enchantment was broken. As dawn broke over the forest, the snow around the castle faded away, the ice melted, and the gardens bloomed to life. In front of the amazed eyes of the villagers, the staff they had been battling became their long-forgotten loved ones. Joyous, spontaneous reunions occurred as memories returned. Mrs. Potts hugged her husband Jean, the potter. Cadenza and Madame de Garderobe embraced with arms that were once more human. Lumiere and Plumette shared a passionate kiss of their own. Even Cogsworth was found by his wife, Madame Clothilde.

My prince and I made our way downstairs, and we were delighted and overwhelmed to see everyone human again as they tearfully embraced one another. Their long nightmare had ended.

It was all over.

Our joy could not be contained to this single moment, of course. With everyone restored to his or her former self, a grand celebration was quickly arranged with all of Villeneuve in attendance. Dancing among the villagers and my friends, in the arms of my prince, I felt more happiness than I can possibly describe—and I saw those same feelings reflected on the faces of everyone around me. Surrounded by music, laughter, and love, it was the most wonderful ending I could have wished for.

Of course, life is not as simple as a storybook, and our story has not yet concluded. Still, our future looks bright and full of even more adventures—adventures my prince and I can choose together. Thus I end my tale with a promise, one I know that I can make come true . .

And they lived happily ever after.

My father has been inspired by places all over the world to create his collection of music boxes.

Writer: Rachael Upton
Editor: Lori Froeb
Designer: Rebecca A. Stone
Copy Editor: Mary Bronzini-Klein
Managing Editor: Christine Guido
Creative Director: Julia Sabbagh
Associate Publisher: Rosanne McManus
Disney Team: Chelsea Alon,
Nachie Marsham, and Brittany Rubiano

Photographs and Illustrations © Disney

Additional images from shutterstock.com: background of all pages © LiliGraphie;
pages 2 and 95 (dried rose) © Marina Kutukova;
pages ii, iii, iv, 2, and 48–55 (white watercolor paper) © David M. Schrader;
pages 11, 26, 39, 41, 43, 44, 78, 85, and 88 (blue paper) © Masyle;
page 5 (old textured white paper) © VL1; page 9 (pressed rose) © CoffeeChocolates;
page 9 (card) © picsfive; pages 9 and 13 (landscape and market illustration) © pavila;
page 15 (flower drawings) © kappacha; pages 33, 96, and 97 (scrap paper) © wanchai;
page 47 (paper for salve recipe) © tanlasneg; page 85 (ink spot) © vadim nardin;
page 89 (rose petals) © Koolapan

Illustrations on pages 5 (village landscape), 25 (beast silhouette), 62 (book),
71 (mirror), and 89 (rose) by Karen Viola

Studio Fun International
An imprint of Printers Row Publishing Group
10350 Barnes Canyon Road, Suite 100, San Diego, CA 92121
www.studiofun.com

Printers Row Publishing Group is a division of
Readerlink Distribution Services, LLC.
Studio Fun International is a registered trademark
of Readerlink Distribution Services, LLC.

All notations of errors or omissions should
be addressed to Studio Fun International,
Editorial Department, at the above address.

ISBN: 978-0-7944-3957-6

Printed and assembled in China.
Conforms to ASTM F963
21 20 19 18 17 1 2 3 4 5
SL2/11/16